THE NOISIEST NIGHT

For Maximouse and Bunjy

OXFORD
UNIVERSITY PRESS

Great Clarendon Street, Oxford OX2 6DP

Oxford University Press is a department of the University of Oxford.
It furthers the University's objective of excellence in research, scholarship,
and education by publishing worldwide in

Oxford New York

Auckland Bangkok Buenos Aires Cape Town Chennai
Dar es Salaam Delhi Hong Kong Istanbul Karachi Kolkata
Kuala Lumpur Madrid Melbourne Mexico City Mumbai Nairobi
São Paulo Shanghai Taipei Tokyo Toronto

Oxford is a registered trade mark of Oxford University Press
in the UK and in certain other countries

Text and illustrations © Thomas Taylor 2007
The moral rights of the author have been asserted

Database right Oxford University Press (maker)

First published 2007

British Library Cataloguing in Publication Data available

ISBN: 978-0-19-272674-2 (hardback)
ISBN: 978-0-19-272675-9 (paperback)
ISBN: 978-0-19-272676-6 (paperback with audio CD)

10 9 8 7 6 5 4 3 2 1

Printed in Thailand by Imago

Thomas Taylor

THE NOISIEST NIGHT

OXFORD
UNIVERSITY PRESS

One evening, as the sun went down, Clovis climbed to the top of a very tall tree. He looked out across the whole jungle for someone to play with but the other animals were already asleep.

Clovis didn't like
being all alone.

Then he saw
something glowing
in the dark.

Fireflies!
'Hello,' said Clovis
to the fireflies.
'I'm being a night-tiger.
Will you play I-spy with me?'

'I spy,' said the first firefly, 'something beginning with P…

with beautiful feathers,

grasping claws,

shiny beaks…'

Then Clovis roared,
'I know, I know,
it's…

Cawr!
Cawr!

Squawk!

'Clovis! Go to bed!'
'Hee hee, let's play again,' said Clovis.

'I spy,' said the next firefly,
'something beginning
with C…

with rough
scaly skin,

small beady eyes,

fearsome jaws

and a
toothsome
surprise.'

'That's easy,' roared
Clovis, 'it's…

Snappety
Snap!

'Clovis, go to bed!'
'But I'm a night-tiger!'
cried Clovis.

'I spy,' said the last firefly,
'something beginning
with E…

with floppy
grey ears,

small whippy tail,

a trumpety trunk,

and tusks long
and pale.'

'I know that too,'
roared Clovis, 'it's…

Braahooha!

Braahooha!

'Clovis, go to bed!'
'But I'm not at all sleepy,' said Clovis.

The fireflies buzzed around Clovis. 'We've seen something else in the jungle tonight,' they said.

'It has terrible claws,

and stamping paws,

spots and
scales,

and feathers too,

and dozens of eyes all
glaring at you. It's...

Squawk!

Snap!
Snap!

Snap!

Oooh!
Oooh!

'Clovis,
will you
please
go to bed!'

'Well I suppose I am
a *bit* sleepy,' yawned
Clovis. 'Good night,
everyone.'

Just then the sun came up.
Clovis the night-tiger settled down
but everyone else was **so noisy**
that it was a very long time indeed
before he got any sleep.

Munch!

Snort!